Eating Out

PUFFIN PIED PIPER BOOKS
Published by the Penguin Group
Penguin Books USA Inc., 375 Hudson Street, New York, New York 10014, U.S.A.
Penguin Books Ltd, 27 Wrights Lane, London W8 5TZ, England
Penguin Books Australia Ltd, Ringwood, Victoria, Australia
Penguin Books Canada Ltd, 10 Alcorn Avenue, Toronto, Ontario, Canada M4V 3B2
Penguin Books (N.Z.) Ltd, 182–190 Wairau Road, Auckland 10, New Zealand
Penguin Books Ltd, Registered Offices: Harmondsworth, Middlesex, England

First published in hardcover in the United States 1983 by
Dial Books for Young Readers
A Division of Penguin Books USA Inc.
Published in Great Britain by Walker Books, Inc.
Copyright © 1983 by Helen Oxenbury
All rights reserved
Library of Congress Catalog Card Number: 82-19802
Printed in Hong Kong
First Puffin Pied Piper Printing 1994
ISBN 0-14-054948-X
1 3 5 7 9 10 8 6 4 2
A Pied Piper Book is a registered trademark of
Dial Books for Young Readers, a division of Penguin Books USA Inc.,
® TM 1,163,686 and ® TM 1,054,312.

Eating Out

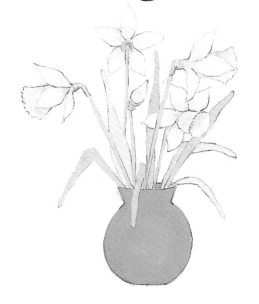

by Helen Oxenbury

A Puffin Pied Piper

Mommy said, "I'm too tired
to cook."
"Me too," said Daddy. "Let's go
out for dinner."

"I suppose you need a high
chair," the waiter said to me.
The room was hot and crowded.

We had to wait and wait for
the food.
"Why can't you sit still like that
nice boy and girl?" Daddy said.

"Get back in your chair,"
Mommy said. "Here comes
your yummy meal."

"Why didn't you say you had
to go before the food came?"
Mommy asked.

I wasn't very hungry, so I went
under the table. Someone
stepped on my foot.

The waiter made a terrible mess.

"That's that," Daddy said.
"Never again," said Mommy.
"Anyway I like eating at home
   the best," I said.

About the Author/Artist

Helen Oxenbury is internationally recognized as one of the finest children's book illustrators, with over thirty books to her credit, including *We're Going on a Bear Hunt* and *The Dragon of an Ordinary Family* (Dial) by Margaret Mahy. Her Very First Books®—five board books for toddlers—have been newly designed and reissued by Dial. According to *The Washington Post,* the books "will delight parents and entertain infants." *The Bulletin of the Center for Children's Books* applauded, "Fun, but more than that: These are geared to the toddler's interests and experiences." Ms. Oxenbury lives in London.